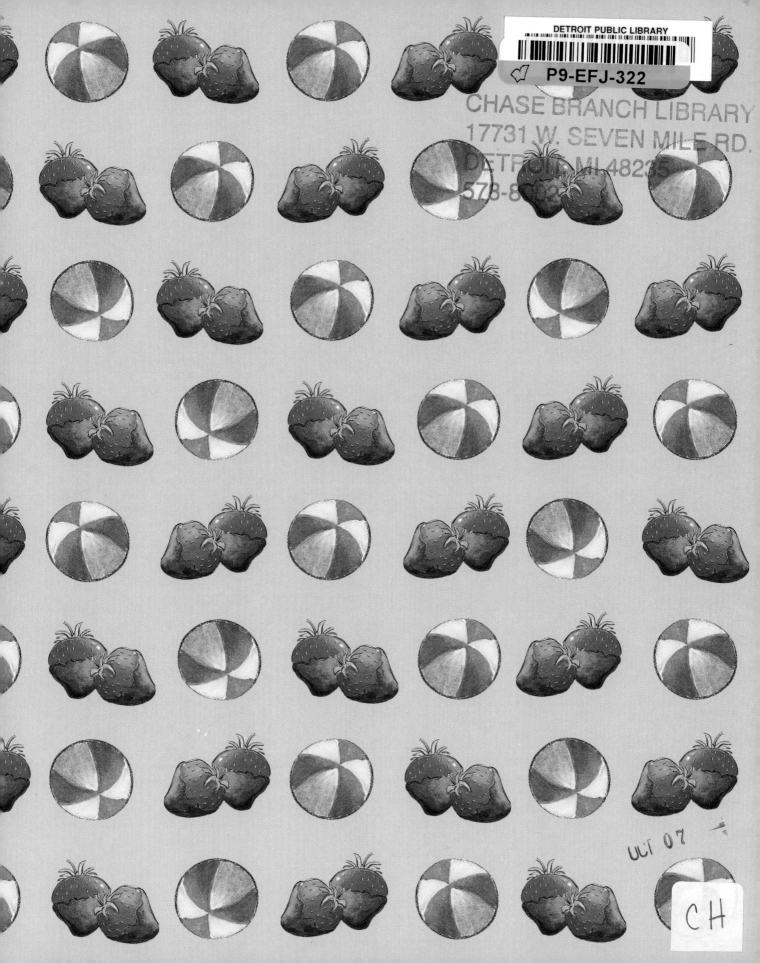

Raymond and Nelda

Written by
Barbara Bottner

Illustrated by
Nancy Hayashi

PEACHTREE
ATLANTA

For Bhagavan and Amma
and all their children —*B. B.*

To Barbara, a great teacher
and friend —*N. H.*

Published by
PEACHTREE PUBLISHERS
1700 Chattahoochee Avenue
Atlanta, Georgia 30318-2112

www.peachtree-online.com

Text © 2007 by Barbara Bottner
Illustrations © 2007 by Nancy Hayashi

ISBN 978-1-56145-394-8

Book design by Nancy Hayashi
Typesetting by Melanie McMahon Ives

Illustrations created in watercolor, pen, and colored pencil.

Printed in Singapore
10 9 8 7 6 5 4 3 2 1
First Edition

Library of Congress Cataloging-in-Publication Data

Bottner, Barbara.
  Raymond and Nelda / written by Barbara Bottner ; illustrated by Nancy Hayashi. -- 1st ed.
     p. cm.
  Summary: Raymond and Nelda have always been the very best of friends, and when they have a falling out they are both so miserable that Florence, their mail carrier, helps them get past their pride and hurt feelings to make up.
  ISBN 978-1-56145-394-8
  [1. Best friends--Fiction. 2. Friendship--Fiction. 3. Letter carriers--Fiction.] I. Hayashi, Nancy, ill. II. Title.
  PZ7.B6586Ray 2007
  [E]--dc22
                              2006024277

Raymond and Nelda were the best of friends.

They made up funny songs together.

You and me,
me and you,
we stick together
as tight as glue.

They ate chocolate-covered strawberries,
even though they were both quite plump.
They tickled each other and laughed until they
couldn't laugh anymore.

They loved to toss Raymond's ball back and forth.

Raymond and Nelda understood each other so well that sometimes they didn't need to say anything.

One day, Nelda twirled for Raymond.

She fell.

Raymond collapsed, giggling.

"Some friend!" said Nelda.

She heaved Raymond's rubber ball into the water.

"I hope you never find it!" she said. And she was gone.

Nelda decided to forget about Raymond.

She read funny books.

She didn't laugh.

She drew pictures.

Bad ones.

She made new friends.

They weren't as much fun as Raymond.

Raymond decided to forget about Nelda.

He watched cartoons.

He didn't laugh.

He rode his bike.

He fell off.

He made new friends.

He thought about Nelda.

"You look like melted butter," Florence the mail
lady told Raymond.

"I'm trying to forget about Nelda," he said.

"Raymond is not the same without you," Florence told Nelda.

"I don't care," said Nelda. "I hope he suffers."

"When he rides his bike, he falls off," said Florence.

"When he reads a book, he can't finish it.

When he tells a joke, he forgets the punch line."

Nelda did not tell Florence that when she played cards,
    she lost every time.
When she went on a walk, the sun hurt her eyes.
And when she told a joke, she couldn't remember the
    punch line.

...and then the cow said uh..... uh.....

Maybe Nelda will call, thought Raymond.

Maybe Raymond will apologize, thought Nelda.

Raymond decided to write a letter to Nelda.

"What should I say?" he asked Florence.

"It's the thought that counts," Florence said.

Raymond was too proud to write this:

"I was a jerk. I miss you."

So instead he wrote this:

Life is just a bowl of cherries... except for the pits.

What did Raymond mean? Nelda wondered.

"Dear Raymond! I am not a pit!" she wrote back to him. "And you are certainly no cherry!"

Raymond didn't know what to say, so he wrote
  another letter.
"It's lonely at the top," it read.

"You think you're the top?" Nelda wrote back.
  "Of what?"

Florence delivered the card to Raymond.
"Some people are better writers than others,"
she told him.

Raymond wrote another letter.

"That's good," said Florence.

Nelda read Raymond's letter. Did he think that nothing was as funny as seeing her fall? How could he be so mean? Nelda wrote, "I think you should find a new best friend! Someone who isn't clumsy would be good."

"If I found a new friend, I wouldn't care if she was clumsy," Raymond replied.
"But she wouldn't throw my ball into the lake."

"He has a point," Florence told Nelda.

Nelda thought about it.

"I'm going to the lake," she said.

She found Raymond's ball.

Raymond decided to be grown up. He bought chocolate-covered strawberries and took the short cut to Nelda's house.

Nelda set out to return Raymond's ball. She took the long way.

Raymond knocked. Nelda wasn't home.

Nelda knocked. Raymond wasn't home.

They bumped smack into each other.

"Here is your ball," said Nelda.

"These are for you," said Raymond.

"I'm not hungry," said Nelda.

"Me neither," said Raymond.

They stared at each other.

"I shouldn't have laughed,"
   said Raymond. "I'm sorry."
"I missed you," Nelda said.
"I hope you'll twirl for me again
   someday," said Raymond.

"You never know," Nelda said.

Raymond and Nelda spent the afternoon
telling each other jokes.
They remembered the punch lines.

They shared the chocolate-covered strawberries with
Florence, the very best mail lady in the world.

And they made up funny songs together.

You and me,

me and you,

we belong together

like socks in a shoe.

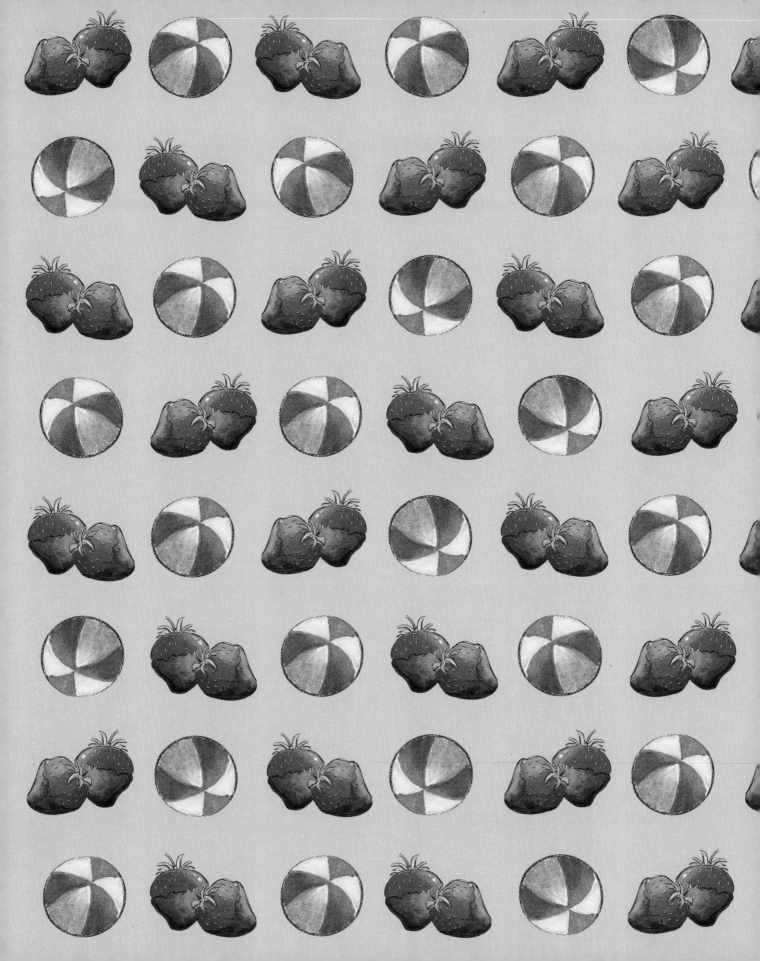